01-C-17-19

P9-DEW-708

A GLUTEN-FREE BIRTHDAY FOR ME!

By Sue Fliess

Illustrated by Jennifer E. Morris

www.av2books.com

Your AV² Media Enhanced book gives you a fiction readalong online. Log on to www.av2books.com and enter the unique book code from this page to use your readalong.

AV² Readalong Navigation

HIGHLIGHTED TEXT HOME 🏠 CLOSE ⊗

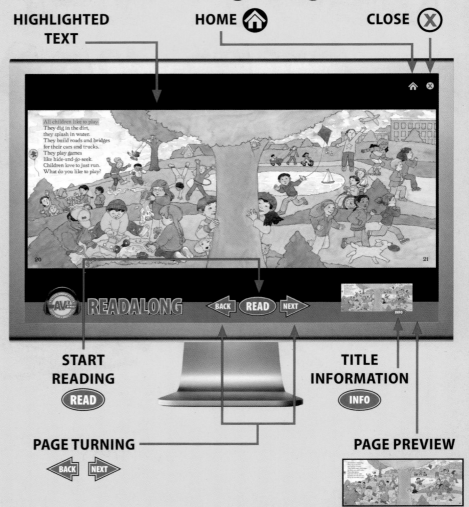

START READING READ

PAGE TURNING BACK NEXT

TITLE INFORMATION INFO

PAGE PREVIEW

Go to **www.av2books.com**, and enter this book's unique code.

BOOK CODE

J808442

AV² by Weigl brings you media enhanced books that support active learning.

First Published by

ALBERT WHITMAN & COMPANY
Publishing children's books since 1919

Published by AV² by Weigl
350 5ᵗʰ Avenue, 59ᵗʰ Floor New York, NY 10118
Websites: www.av2books.com   www.weigl.com

Copyright ©2015 AV² by Weigl

Printed in the United States of America in North Mankato, Minnesota
1 2 3 4 5 6 7 8 9 0 18 17 16 15 14

042014
WEP080414

Library of Congress Control Number: 2014937590

ISBN 978-1-4896-2326-3 (hardcover)
ISBN 978-1-4896-2327-0 (single user eBook)
ISBN 978-1-4896-2328-7 (multi-user eBook)

Text copyright ©2013 by Sue Fliess.
Illustrations copyright ©2013 by Jennifer E. Morris.
Published in 2013 by Albert Whitman & Company.

It's my birthday...

3

I can't wait!
Time for us to celebrate!

House is ready, set for fun.
Cake's the last thing, then
we're done.

5

Can't use flour,
can't eat wheat...
That's got gluten! What's to eat?

GLUTEN
FREE
GRUB

GLUTEN FREE
GRUB

Eat
without
Wheat

NEW!

Search the cookbooks...
time to bake—
chocolate-cookie-crumble cake!

START

8

Guests arriving, games begin.
Relay races, who will win?

9

Painting faces,
fake tattoos,
dragons, fairies, I can't choose!

11

Mom yells, "Cake time!" We all dash. Candles flicker, cameras flash.

12

Wait a minute...
Someone's gone...
Sitting sadly on the lawn.

13

"Don't you want some?
It tastes good."
He says, "I sure wish I could.

Can't have gluten.
Can't eat cake,
gives me such a tummy ache."

"I'm the same way!
Come and see—
my cake's sweet and gluten-free!"

Friends are singing,
what's my wish?
Hope the crumble cake's delish!

"Cake is yummy!"
"We want more!"
"Did they bake it at the store?"

"Nope, we made it.
Icing too.
Wasn't all that hard to do."

Open presents,
thank my friends.
Party favors...party ends.

23

Guests are leaving.
Wave good-bye...

24

Next year we'll make ice-cream pie!

Chocolate-Cookie-Crumble Cake
16 Servings

INGREDIENTS:

2 cups gluten-free all-purpose flour (Maninis)

1 cup white sugar

1 cup dark brown sugar

3/4 cup unsweetened cocoa powder

1 teaspoon baking powder 1 teaspoon salt

1 teaspoon ground cinnamon

1/2 cup water

1/2 cup brewed decaf coffee (don't worry, it doesn't give a coffee taste!)

1 cup coconut oil

2 teaspoons vanilla extract

a few of your favorite gluten-free cookies (optional)

DIRECTIONS:

Preheat oven to 350 °F.

In a large bowl, stir together the flour, sugars, cocoa powder, baking powder, salt, and cinnamon. Pour in water, coffee, coconut oil, and vanilla; mix until blended well.

Spread evenly in a 9 x 13 inch baking pan or spoon into mini-muffin pans filling each cup three quarters of the way.

Bake for 20–25 minutes in the baking pan or 12–15 minutes in the mini-muffin pans. If desired, crumble your favorite gluten-free cookies on top while cake is still warm. Let cool on wire rack in pans for at least 10 minutes before cutting into squares (if using the baking pan) or removing from the mini-muffin pans.

Very Berry Pie with Ice Cream
8 Servings

INGREDIENTS:

Filling:

4 cups fresh or frozen mixed berries (blueberries, raspberries, black-berries, strawberries)

1/2 cup sugar

2 tablespoons lemon juice 2 tablespoons tapioca starch 1 teaspoon vanilla extract

1 teaspoon ground cinnamon

Topping:

1/4 cup unsalted butter or coconut oil melted

1 cup gluten-free rolled oats (Bob's Red Mill)

1/2 cup gluten-free all-purpose flour (Maninis)

1/2 cup dark brown sugar

1 teaspoon salt

1/2 teaspoon ground cinnamon gluten-free ice cream to serve

DIRECTIONS:

Preheat oven to 375 °F.

In a large bowl, stir together the berries, sugar, lemon juice, tapioca starch, vanilla, and cinnamon. Spread evenly in a 9 x 13 inch baking pan.

In a separate bowl, stir together the butter or coconut oil, oats, flour, brown sugar, salt, and cinnamon. Spread evenly over the berries in the baking pan.

Bake for 35–40 minutes in the baking pan until berries are bubbling vigorously.

Remove from oven and let cool on wire rack in pans for at least 1 hour before serving.

Top slices of pie with a big scoop (or two) of your favorite gluten-free ice cream!

Tips for friends and family with gluten allergies

What is gluten anyway?

Gluten is a protein found in wheat, barley, and rye. It's what makes dough stretchy, helps it to rise and keep shape, and often gives foods their chewy texture.

Did you know?
Gluten is sticky. The word *gluten* comes from Latin, meaning "glue"!

Can't have gluten? Here are some helpful tips for being gluten-free:

* Focus on what your child can eat, not what he or she can't eat.
* Make it fun—let your kids be part of the menu-planning and cooking process.
* Keep your child's classroom stocked with a gluten-free snack, such as fruit gummies, for class parties when treats that contain gluten are provided. That way your child knows ahead of time that he, too, will have a yummy treat during the party.
* When dining out, call the restaurant and check the menu ahead of time. Often the restaurant will have their menu available to view online. If it does not, explain your situation to the manager when you arrive and make sure they are willing to work with you.

* Be careful of soy. When looking for food made without gluten, often products will replace gluten with soy. However, soy can often be cross-contaminated by wheat and may contain gluten. This goes for oats too. Oats are often grown in rotation with gluten crops.

* Look for a certified gluten-free seal on food products. So many products now carry these labels that it's become easier to find these foods. Gluten-free certification programs require food manufacturers to follow strict sourcing guidelines for their raw materials, which means the end products will contain less cross-contamination too.

* There are many great substitutes for regular flour including rice flour, corn flour, flaxseed flour, and more.

* Make sure your allergic child doesn't borrow a sibling's or a friend's utensils to avoid accidentally eating gluten.

* When washing dishes, use separate sponges for gluten-free and gluten dishes.

* Whether your child is gluten intolerant or not, when hosting a party for your child, avoid all treats that could be problematic and give out balloons instead!

Helpful websites and resources

celiac.com/gluten-free

A celiac disease and

gluten-free forum

celiaccentral.org/kids

celiacdisease.about.com

eatingglutenfree.com

glutenfreely.com

glutenfreeville.com

glutenfreeworks.com

fda.gov *Provides information about food labeling*